THE
HAIR
BOOK

latonya yvette &
amanda jane jones

STERLING CHILDREN'S BOOKS
New York

long hair

short hair

mustache hair

monster hair!

cornrow hair

covered hair

cap hair

kippah hair

party hair

beard hair

bun hair

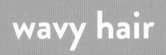

windy hair

afro hair

all gone hair!

No matter your hair . . .

You are welcome